A DINOSAUR LIVES IN MY HOUSE ™

Written by Nora Smith
Illustrated by Gary Albright

Copyright © 1988 Marvel Entertainment Group, Inc. All rights
reserved. Marvel Monkey Tales, A Dinosaur Lives in My House
(including all prominent characters appearing herein) and the
distinctive likenesses thereof are trademarks of Marvel
Entertainment Group, Inc.
ISBN 0-87135-371-7

Watch out! There's a dinosaur in my house. It's not an ordinary dinosaur. It's a magic dinosaur, and I am the dinosaur's magician.

I can make my dinosaur change shapes. I can turn it into any dinosaur I want. All I have to say are the magic words.

If I want some dinosaur eggs for breakfast,
I say,

"The next dinosaur
You will be
Is Oviraptor—
Just for me."

If I want to measure myself against the biggest
dinosaur of all, I say:

"The next dinosaur
You will be
Is Supersaurus—
Just for me."

If I want to race a dinosaur that's smaller than me, I say:

"The next dinosaur
You will be
Is little Mussaurus—
Just for me."

If I want to slide down a long slide, I say,

"The next dinosaur
You will be
Is Diplodocus—
Just for me."

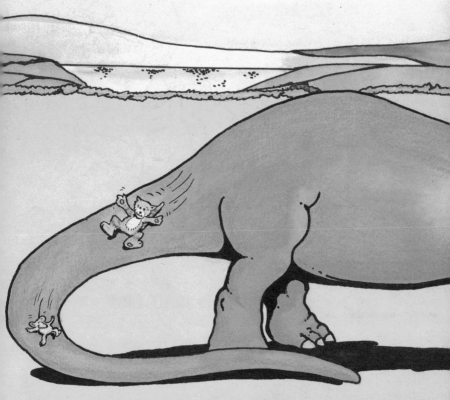

If I want to play ring toss, I say:

"The next dinosaur
You will be
Is Triceratops—
Just for me."

If I want to climb up an new, interesting
climbing gym, I say:

"The next dinosaur
You will be
Is Stegosaurus—
Just for me."

If I want to shovel up plants from the bottom of a pond, I say,

"The next dinosaur
You will be
Is Anatosaurus—
Just for me."

If I want to go swimming, I say,

"The next dinosaur
You will be
Is Ichthyosaurus—
Just for me."

If I want to scare off a bully, I say,

"The next dinosaur
You will be
Is Tyrannosaurus Rex—
Just for me."

If I want to reach the tops of trees, I say,

"The next dinosaur
You will be
Is Brontosaurus—
Just for me."

If I want to knock down bushes to make a path
to the mountain, I say,

"The next dinosaur
You will be
Is Ankylosaurus—
Just for me."

If I want to fly to the clouds, I say,

"The next dinosaur
You will be
Is Pteranodon—
Just for me."

If I want my dinosaur to be soft and cuddly,
I say,

"The next dinosaur
You will be
Is Pillosaurus—
Just for me."